E
S
c.2

Smucker, Anna
Egan.
No star nights

NO STAR NIGHTS

by Anna Egan Smucker
paintings by Steve Johnson

Alfred A. Knopf · New York

THIS IS A BORZOI BOOK
PUBLISHED BY ALFRED A. KNOPF, INC.

Text copyright © 1989 by Anna Egan Smucker
Illustrations copyright © 1989 by Steve Johnson
All rights reserved under International and Pan-American Copyright
Conventions. Published in the United States by Alfred A. Knopf, Inc.,
New York, and simultaneously in Canada by Random House of
Canada Limited, Toronto. Distributed by Random House, Inc., New York.
Manufactured in Singapore
Book design by Elizabeth Hardie

2 4 6 8 0 9 7 5 3

Library of Congress Cataloging-in-Publication Data
Smucker, Anna Egan. No star nights. Summary: A young girl
growing up in a steel mill town in the 1950s describes her
childhood and how it was affected by the local industry.
[1. Steel industry and trade—Fiction]
I. Johnson, Steve, 1960–   ill. II. Title.
PZ7.S66478No   1988   [E]   88-2782
ISBN 0-394-89925-3 ISBN 0-394-99925-8 (lib. bdg.)

For the Kucans, the Pottersnaks,
and the other steelworker families whose
children I grew up with
A. E. S.

For Bruce and Donna Johnson,
and Paul and Mary Fancher
S. J.

When I was little, we couldn't see the stars in the nighttime sky because the furnaces of the mill turned the darkness into a red glow. But we would lie on the hill and look up at the sky anyway and wait for a bright orange light that seemed to breathe in and out to spread across it. And we would know that the golden spark-spitting steel was being poured out of giant buckets into molds to cool.

Then we would look down on a train pulling cars mounted with giant thimbles rocking back and forth. They were filled with fiery hot molten slag that in the night glowed orange. And when they were dumped, the sky lit up again.

A loud steam whistle that echoed off the hills announced the change of shifts, and hundreds of men streamed out of the mill's gates. Everyone's dad worked in the mill, and carried a tin lunchbox and a big metal thermos bottle.

Work at the mill went on night and day. When Dad worked

night shift, we children had to whisper and play quietly during the day so that we didn't wake him up. His job was too dangerous for him to go without sleep. He operated a crane that lifted heavy ingots of steel into a pit that was thousands of degrees hot.

When Dad worked the three-to-eleven shift, Mom made dinner early so we could all eat together. She made the best stuffed cabbage of anyone in the neighborhood. We sometimes tried to help fold the cabbage leaves around the meat and rice like she did, but our cabbage leaves always came unrolled.

During the school year days went by when we didn't see Dad at all because he was either at work or sleeping. When he changed shifts from daylight to night and back again it took him a while to get used to the different waking and sleeping times. We called these his grumpy times. We liked it best when he had daylight hours to spend with us. We played baseball until it was too dark to see the ball.

On a few very special summer afternoons he would load us all into the car for a hot, sweaty trip to Pittsburgh and a doubleheader Pirates game at Forbes Field. We sat in the bleachers way out in left field, eating popcorn and drinking lemonade that we brought from home, yelling our heads off for the Pirates. Our brother always wore his baseball glove, hoping to catch a foul ball that might come into the stands. Dad helped us mark our scorecards and bought us hot dogs during the seventh-inning stretch.

On our way home we passed the black silhouettes of Pittsburgh's steel mills, with their great heavy clouds of smoke billowing from endless rows of smokestacks. The road wound along as the river wound, and between us and the river were the

mills, and on the other side of the road were the hills—the river, the mills, and the hills. And we sang as we rode home, "She'll be comin' round the mountain when she comes..."

July was just about the best month of the year. Everyone who
worked in the mill got their vacation pay then. We called it
Christmas in July. All the stores had big sales. Even though it
wasn't really Christmas, we each got a present.

And the Fourth of July parade was something everyone looked forward to. We were busy for weeks making flowers out of Kleenex to cover our Girl Scout float. Some of our friends took baton lessons and were part of a marching unit called the Steel Town Strutters. They wore shiny black-and-gold-spangled leotards and threw their batons high up into the air and caught them! Something we sure couldn't do. But our favorites were the baby strutters. Some of them were only two years old. They did a good job just carrying their batons.

With all the bands and fire engines and floats, the parade went
on and on. There were convertibles with beauty queens sitting on
the back. Members of the Kennel Club marched their dogs in
circles and figure eights. Kids rode bikes decorated with colored

crepe paper, flags, and balloons. The mayor drove an old-fashioned car, and his children threw bubblegum and candies into the crowds.

We went to school across from the mill. The smokestacks towered above us and the smoke billowed out in great puffy clouds of red, orange, and yellow, but mostly the color of rust. Everything—houses, hedges, old cars—was a rusty red color. Everything but the little bits of graphite, and they glinted like silver in the dust. At recess when the wind whirled these sharp, shiny metal pieces around, we girls would crouch so that our skirts touched the ground and kept our bare legs from being stung.

We would squint our eyes when the wind blew to keep the graphite out. Once a piece got caught in my eye, and no matter how much I blinked or how much my eye watered it wouldn't come out. When the eye doctor finally took it out and showed it to me, I was amazed that a speck that small could feel so big.

We played on the steep street that ran up the hill beside our school. Our favorite game was dodge ball. The kids on the bottom row knew they had to catch the ball. If they didn't, it would roll down onto the busy county road that ran in front of the school. Too often a truck carrying a heavy roll of steel would run over it and with a loud *bang* the ball would be flattened.

The windows in our school were kept closed to try to keep the graphite and smoke out. On really windy days we could hear the dry, dusty sound of grit hitting against the glass. Dusting the room was a daily job. The best duster got to dust the teacher's

desk with a soft white cloth and a spray that made the whole
room smell like lemons. It was always a mystery to us how the
nuns who were our teachers could keep the white parts of their
habits so clean.

Some days it seemed as though there was a giant lid covering
the valley, keeping the smoke in. It was so thick you couldn't see

anything clearly. On days like that I felt as if we were living in a
whirling world of smoke.

The road we took home from school went right through part of the mill. Tall cement walls with strands of barbed wire at the top kept us on the sidewalk and out of the mill. But when we got to the bridge that spanned the railroad tracks, there was just a steel mesh fence. From there we could look straight down into the mill! There was always something wonderful to watch. Through a huge open doorway we could see the mammoth open-hearth furnace. A giant ladle would tilt to give the fiery furnace a "drink" of orange, molten iron. Sometimes we would see the golden, liquid steel pouring out the bottom of the open hearth into enormous bucketlike ladles. The workers were just small dark figures made even smaller by the great size of the ladles and the furnace. The hot glow of the liquid steel made the dark mill light up as if the sun itself was being poured out. And standing on the bridge we could feel its awful heat.

Warning sirens and the toots of steam whistles, the screeching sounds of train wheels and the wham-wham of cars being coupled and uncoupled—all these sounds surrounded us as we stood on the bridge. From the other side we could look into another part of the mill. Rows of lights hung from girders across the ceiling. White-hot steel bars glided smoothly over rollers on long tables. Men were using torches on the big slabs of steel. The torches gave off streaks of burning, white light and showers of sparks that looked like our Fourth of July sparklers.

Behind the mill rose huge
piles of black shiny coal and rich
red iron ore, and a hill of rusting
scrap metal. A crane that to us
looked like a dinosaur with huge
jaws was constantly at work
picking up twisted, jagged pieces
of metal and dropping them
into railroad cars to be taken into
the mill. Sometimes we would
imagine that the mill itself was
a huge beast, glowing hot,
breathing heavily, always hungry,
always needing to be fed. And we
would run home, not stopping
once to look back over our
shoulders.

Not too far from our house was a hill made of boulders of slag from the mill. Our grandfather told us that long ago it had been a deep ravine. Over the years truckload after truckload of slag from the mill had been dumped into it until the hole had become a hill. Now it towered over the old houses that were near it.

For an adventure, my best friend and I once decided to climb the slag hill. We slipped and slid and sent the pitted rocks rolling down as we scrambled up. Our younger sisters spied us, by now near the top, and started climbing too. It was then that my friend and I saw the dump truck with a heavy load of slag from the mill slowly winding its way up the hill.

"Don't dump! Don't dump!" we screamed. But the deep
engine sounds of the truck straining under its great load drowned
out our cries. Chunks of slag fell onto the roadway. The truck
backed onto the flat place to dump its load. Stumbling toward it,
we waved our arms and screamed again, "Don't dump! Please

don't dump! Our sisters are down there!" The driver finally heard us, and leaning out the window of the cab he saw the little girls. He nodded and waved his hand, then the truck lurched forward back onto the road and disappeared around the curve.

We sank exhausted to the ground, our hearts pounding in our ears. The roar of the truck's engine became fainter and fainter. The sky around us was turning red and orange and gold. We looked down on the mill that seemed to go on forever into the

valley. From its long straight row of stacks, clouds of orange smoke swirled into the colors of the sunset. In the distance a whistle blew.

Many years have passed since then, and now the slag hill is covered with grasses and blackberry bushes and sumac trees. The night sky is clear and star filled because the mill is shut down. The big buckets no longer pour the hot, yellow steel. The furnaces whose fires lit up everything are rusting and cold.

Not many children live in the town now. Most of the younger people have moved away to other places to find work. The valley's steelworking way of life is gone forever. But whenever the grandchildren come back to visit, they love more than anything else to listen to stories about the days when all night long the sky glowed red.

ANNA EGAN SMUCKER was born in Steubenville, Ohio, and grew up in Weirton, West Virginia, the steel-mill town that is the setting for *No Star Nights*. She graduated with a degree in English from Carlow College in Pittsburgh and later earned an M.A. from Michigan State University in East Lansing. A former elementary school teacher, she currently works as a children's librarian in Clarksburg, West Virginia. She lives not far away in Bridgeport, with her husband and two children. This is her first book.

STEVE JOHNSON was born in White Bear Lake, Minnesota, and earned a B.F.A. in illustration from the School of Associated Arts in St. Paul. He has won many illustration awards, and his work has been exhibited in several national shows—as well as a 1985 tour of China. He works in close collaboration with his creative associate, Lou Fancher. *No Star Nights* is his first children's book. Johnson is married and lives in Minneapolis.